DRACULA'S
DAUGHTER

This edition first published in Great Britain in 1999 by Mammoth
First published in Great Britain 1988 by Heinemann Young Books
imprints of Egmont Children's Books Limited
239 Kensington High Street, London W8 6SA.
Published in hardback by Heinemann Library,
a division of Reed Educational and Professional Publishing Limited
by arrangement with Egmont Children's Books Limited.
Text copyright © Mary Hoffman 1988
Illustrations copyright © Chris Riddell 1988
Additional illustrations copyright © Chris Riddell 1999
The Author and Illustrator have asserted their moral rights.
Paperback ISBN 0 7497 3582 1
Hardback ISBN 0 431 06196 3
10 9 8 7 6 5 4 3 2 1
A CIP catalogue record for this title
is available from the British Library.
Printed at Oriental Press Limited, Dubai.

Mary Hoffman

DRACULA'S DAUGHTER

Illustrated by Chris Riddell

 YELLOW BANANAS

For Ertaç and the
other Lea Valley juniors who
encouraged me to finish it
M.H.

For Katy
C.R.

Chapter One

ANGELA WAS A model child in every way. Of course her arrival was unusual. Mr and Mrs Batty were not expecting a baby – they were expecting a parcel of plants they had ordered for the garden. So they weren't surprised when there was a ring at the doorbell and a basket dumped on the step. Only in the basket was a baby girl with brown eyes and black hair. Mr and Mrs Batty forgot all about the plants and looked after the baby instead.

She looked such a little angel, they decided to call her Angela. On the first anniversary of her arrival through the post, the baby was adopted and became Angela Batty. There were no problems in her babyhood. She walked and talked on time, ate up her greens, tidied up after her games and did not pull the cat's tail.

The trouble really began on her fifth birthday. In the bundle with Angela there had been an envelope saying:

"This child was born on 31st October. Open this letter on her 5th birthday."

Of course, Mr and Mrs Batty had wanted to open the envelope straight away, in case it contained a clue about her parents, but they somehow felt it would be unlucky to look inside before the given date. So after Angela's birthday party, when all her friends had gone home clutching their loot bags, her parents solemnly took down the envelope and opened it.

That was all. Mr and Mrs Batty were a bit disappointed and they rather objected to this grand lady referring to Angela as 'her' daughter.

'She's ours now – all legal,' said Mrs Batty firmly.

'Besides,' said her husband, 'if she was a rich lady, as it seems, why did she have to go dumping her child on a doorstep?'

For a while everything went on as normal. Angela went to school, made friends and was called a good girl by her teachers. Several of her friends began to get wobbly teeth and talk about the tooth fairy and ten pences. So Angela's parents were not surprised when she got her first gap. But, when the new tooth grew to fill the gap, they *were* a bit worried. All the other children had nice square teeth, but

Angela's came to a sharp point, like a shark's.
The dentist was puzzled, but not really worried
– he reckoned Angela's tooth could be filed
straight when she was older. But even he
declared himself beaten by the time Angela
was in top infants and had a mouthful of sharp
pointed teeth.

Some of Angela's old friends were no longer allowed to come and play at her house, their parents didn't like the look of those fangs.

Other odd things had started to happen too. Angela had always been good about eating her vegetables, but now she became almost entirely a meat-eater. She loved beefburgers, chops, roast Sunday joints and steaks if she could get them. She would tuck happily into the sort of meat that other children didn't enjoy, like liver and kidney. She also enjoyed beetroot, blackcurrant juice, red cabbage and raspberries.

When Mr and Mrs Batty saw their beloved daughter lifting her smiling face from a bowlful of raspberries, with her pointed teeth stained all red, they exchanged nervous looks.

Other strange things happened too. Mrs Batty took a course in French cookery and began to be adventurous about sauces. But the day she came home with her first bunch of garlic,

Angela let out a scream and hid in the garden shed. She wouldn't come back indoors until Mrs Batty had thrown the garlic out. The Battys hadn't got Angela christened as a baby and now they were beginning to wonder if that would help. They invited the vicar round one afternoon. All went well until Angela came in from school. She took one look at his dog-collar and cross and ran for the shed again.

The mystery was settled once and for all that evening. After Angela had gone to bed, Mr and Mrs Batty got out the envelope and read the card inside it again. Mr Batty had been doing the crossword in the newspaper and now he pointed to the signature with a shaking finger.

'My dear – it's an anagram. Mix up the letters in CLARA DU COTUN and what do you get? COUNT DRACULA!'

Chapter Two

IT DIDN'T TAKE the Battys long to get used to having a vampire in the family. After all, Angela didn't show any signs of wanting to bite anyone. But one thing her parents had definitely decided was that if her original father ever *did* turn up, they would not let him take her away from them.

'If she *is* a vampire,' said Mrs Batty, which was a thing she never talked about except to Mr Batty, 'at least if she stays with us she will be a nice well brought up vampire, who brushes her teeth after every meal.'

But the teeth weren't the only problem. It was an unusually warm autumn and the Battys left the bedroom windows open all night to cool the house down. One night Mr Batty could not sleep for the heat and he went to look in on Angela. He was back in his own bedroom in a flash, shaking his wife awake.

'Wake up, my dear!' he shouted, 'she's gone! Angela's not there!'

But when Mrs Batty had woken up and run down the corridor, she found Angela sleeping peacefully in her bed, with her usual angelic smile.

'You must have been dreaming,' she told her husband crossly, 'waking me up and frightening me for nothing like that!' But she closed Angela's window all the same.

October came in as warm as September and the Battys began to prepare for Angela's seventh birthday party. She had asked for a proper Hallowe'en party, with dressing up, a cauldron cake and pumpkin lanterns at the windows. Her parents were nervous – it seemed to them to be asking for trouble. On the other hand, lots of normal children were going to Hallowe'en parties too.

'It's bound to appeal to her nature,' said Mr Batty. 'Angela being what we think she is. But she's a good girl. I don't think she can be *all* vampire, you know.'

Angela certainly looked all vampire on the night. She wore a short black cloak that Mrs Batty had made for her, and had circled her eyes with red lipstick. She had rubbed green eye shadow – bought specially – all over her face. When she smiled her fangy little smile, her parents couldn't help shuddering.

'I do hope we're doing the right thing with this party,' said Mrs Batty, as Angela rushed to open the door. She let in another vampire, two witches, an imp and a wizard.

'You look terrific, Angela!' said one of the
witches, who was her friend Emma from
school, 'Really scary!'

After they had been joined by some more vampires and a spook or two, the party really got going. As the games were played and prizes won, most of the children acquired long red fingernails or white plastic fangs. Angela began to look just like everyone else. The house had a pumpkin lantern at every window and even Mrs Batty wore a tall black hat. So they were visited by a specially large number of trick-or-treat gangs that night. Mrs Batty was prepared, with a big bowl of currant-cakes she had made, right by the front door.

So when the doorbell rang yet again, she already had a cake in her hand as she opened the door to a tall black-haired man in an opera cloak, who looked just like Count Dracula.

Chapter Three

'GOOD EVENING!' SAID the man who looked like Count Dracula. 'Can I come in?'

Mrs Batty stood frozen in the hall, the cake in her hand. Just then her husband popped his head out of the living room.

'Oh good,' he said, 'I see the entertainer's here. Dressed for the part too! Come in then Mr . . . er?'

'Count,' said the man.

'Mr Count,' said Mr Batty, 'the children are all ready for you.'

"Mr Count" gave a ghastly smile and walked into the Batty's living room. Mrs Batty watched silently in horror, unable to move or speak. The cat streaked through the hall and out through the front door. Mrs Batty automatically closed it and went into the living room. The children were wild about the entertainer.

'Coo, Angela,' said her friend Darren, 'he isn't half realistic. Looks just like the real thing! Watch out for your neck!'

The entertainer didn't tell jokes or do tricks.

But every time he spoke or looked at the children they cheered and laughed. All except Angela. She was watching him with a queer look in her eye. And Mrs Batty was watching her.

"Mr Count" was watching everyone. He hadn't thought it would be so hard to recognise his own daughter, but all these little humans looked like vampires to him.

When he said, 'Who wants to come with me to my castle?' all the children put up their hands and shouted 'Me! Me!' Except one. And that one really *did* look like a vampire – the teeth were very natural, even though all that green stuff was obviously false.

The doorbell rang again. Mrs Batty saw the tall dark stranger moving towards her beloved daughter and felt something snap inside her. 'Angela!' she shrieked as she rushed between them.

The man turned on her with flashing eyes and fangs bared. He looked as if he was going to sink them into her plump pink neck. The children went very quiet and then there was a rustling sound. Angela had spread out her arms under her black cloak and flapped steadily up to the ceiling.

The "entertainer" took his eyes off Mrs Batty to watch his daughter proudly as she swooped round the room. Mr Batty was nowhere to be seen. Mrs Batty picked up a plastic sword that the "wizard" had brought and held it upside down in the shape of a cross, right in front of the man in the black cloak.

'If only I had some garlic,' she muttered.

'Come down, Fangella!' called the tall dark man. 'I've come to take you home. I see you are a credit to me.'

'Over my dead body!' cried Mrs Batty angrily, waving the plastic sword.

The man flinched, but said menacingly, 'That could be arranged.'

'Oh no you don't,' said Angela firmly, hanging upside down from the lampshade.

'I don't want to go to your horrid damp old castle with its spiders and rats. I want to stay here, where there's central heating and a nice cuddly cat.'

'But Fangella, you are my daughter!'

'Don't you dare call her that,' yelled Mrs Batty. 'Her name is *Angela* and she is my daughter now! She's adopted.' She took the adoption certificate, which she always carried in her pocket and waved it in the tall man's face, never letting go of the sword.

'She's not a Dopted, she's a Vampire!' shouted the man. 'I left her here nearly seven years ago, when I – er – had to go away for a while. And now I've come back to collect her.'

'I'm not going,' said Angela. 'You tried to bite my mother!'

The man gave a nasty laugh.

'I *did* bite your mother, Fangella, long ago. She was another one just like this, but she turned out to be too tough for me.'

Angela gasped. 'You mean I'm only *half a vampire?*'

'Yes, but your mother got away when I stole you and found some other human to help her. Between them they had me followed and locked up in a crypt with a strong spell on the door. I couldn't escape till your mother died. She never found out where I left you and now I claim you as my own. It's a vampire's father that really matters – by the way where *is* that silly human that thought I was a party magician?'

Angela looked round wildly for Mr Batty but he wasn't there. The other children were all looking up at Angela on the ceiling with their mouths open.

'I'm not going,' said Angela again. 'I'm only half a vampire and I'm going to choose to be the other half.'

'We'll see about that,' said the tall man. 'Just you wait till I get my fangs on you.' Then he spread his cloak and aimed himself at the lampshade.

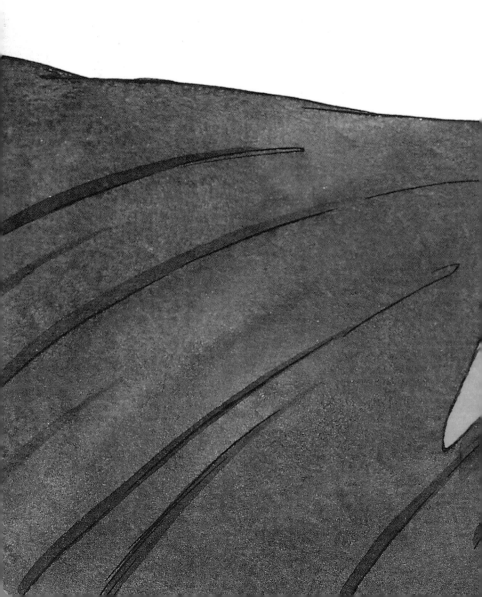

Chapter Four

AS HE LAUNCHED himself up towards Angela,
the man in black suddenly gave a loud scream
and fell to the ground at the sight of Mr Batty,
in the doorway, holding a large tree with
orange berries on its branches and earth
dropping from its roots. Behind him stood
another tall man in evening dress.

'Gotcha, you daft old bat!' said Mr Batty triumphantly, and prodded the cloaked figure with the tree. The shrieks and moans became louder. 'We don't want you or any of your kind ever coming to bother our Angela again! This is a rowan tree and I know you vampires can't bear them. I'm going down to the garden centre tomorrow to buy up their whole stock and I'm going to plant them all round the house!

Now be off with you!' Mr Batty motioned to the window and Mrs Batty opened it.

The man who looked just like Count Dracula dragged himself up onto the window-ledge and sat hunched there with his black cloak drooping down like a tattered old umbrella.

'So this is all the thanks I get,' he hissed up at Angela. 'A fine vampire you've turned out to be!'

'Half vampire,' corrected Angela, still upside down.

'Very well,' he said, 'stay here and eat your rice-pudding and go to Sunday school and knit the cat a pair of bootees if that's what you  want. You'll never get another chance like this. You would have had a much more exciting life with me!' Then he launched himself out of the window and flapped away into the night. Angela landed neatly on the floor right way up and gave a bow.

'Come on, dear,' whispered Mr Batty, putting down his tree and starting to clap. Mrs Batty got the message and clapped loudly. Soon all the children were clapping and cheering wildly.

'That was really *wicked*, Angela,' said Darren admiringly. 'How did you do the flying bit? And who *was* that geezer?'

'Oh just a distant relation on a flying visit,' giggled Angela.

'I'll never forget tonight,' said Mrs Batty, when the guests had all gone home and she and her husband were drinking their cocoa.

'When did you realise he wasn't the entertainer?'

'When I let the real one in, of course,' said Mr Batty. 'He caught on really quickly and helped me dig up the rowan.'

'That *was* a bit of luck,' said Mrs Batty. 'I didn't know we had a rowan tree in the garden.'

'We didn't,' said Mr Batty grimly, 'I pinched it from next door's garden. I expect they'll think it was the trick-or-treaters.'

'Well it would be hard to explain why you'd done it,' said his wife. 'But I'm really proud of you – and of Angela.'

'And I'm proud of you love, facing that old Count with nothing but a plastic sword.'

'You know one thing though, dear,' said Mrs Batty, 'he made me think it might be a bit dull for Angela living with us. We *are* a bit set in our ways.'

'Still, she chose us didn't she?' said her husband, licking the cocoa froth from his lips. 'She can't think we're too boring. But I'll try to be more adventurous if you like. What do you want me to do?'

'How about a nice holiday?' said Mrs Batty. 'We could go somewhere a bit different at Christmas.'

Mr Batty smiled. 'All right, dear. You get some brochures and we'll take our Angela off to somewhere exotic. Only mind – nowhere near Transylvania!'

Yellow Bananas are bright, funny, brilliantly imaginative stories written by some of today's top writers. All the books are beautifully illustrated in full colour.

So if you've enjoyed this story, why not pick another from the bunch?

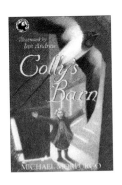

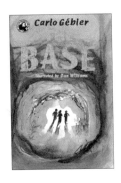